Alfred Durlacher

Western Australia - Report on the General Statistics of the Colony, for the Year 1859

Anatiposi

Alfred Durlacher

Western Australia - Report on the General Statistics of the Colony, for the Year 1859

Reprint of the original, first published in 1859.

1st Edition 2023 | ISBN: 978-3-38230-944-2

Anatiposi Verlag is an imprint of Outlook Verlagsgesellschaft mbH.

Verlag (Publisher): Outlook Verlag GmbH, Zeilweg 44, 60439 Frankfurt, Deutschland
Vertretungsberechtigt (Authorized to represent): E. Roepke, Zeilweg 44, 60439 Frankfurt, Deutschland
Druck (Print): Books on Demand GmbH, In de Tarpen 42, 22848 Norderstedt, Deutschland

CAUSES of DEATH in six years from 1st January, 1854, to 31st December, 1859.

DISEASE AND CAUSE OF DEATH	Under 1			1 to 3			3 to 5			Total under 5			5 to 15			15 to 20			20 to 30			30 to 40			40 to 50			50 to 60			60 and upwards			Total 5 and upwards			GRAND TOTAL		
	Males	Females	Total	Males	Females	Total	Males	Females	Total	Males	Females	Total	Males	Females	Total	Males	Females	Total	Males	Females	Total	Males	Females	Total	Males	Females	Total	Males	Females	Total	Males	Females	Total	Males	Females	Total	Males	Females	Total
Anasarca																																							
Accident																																							
Atrophy																																							
Abscess																																							
Asthma																																							
Apoplexy																																							
Ague																																							
Brain, disease of																																							
Bowel, disease of																																							
Bladder and Kidneys																																							
Burns																																							
Croup																																							
Convulsions																																							
Cancer																																							
Child Birth																																							
Dropsy																																							
Decline																																							
Diarrhœa																																							
Debility																																							
Delirium Tremens																																							
Epilepsy																																							
Fever																																							
Hæmorrhage																																							
Hooping Cough																																							
Heart, disease of																																							
Lungs, disease of																																							
Liver																																							
Lock Jaw																																							
Malformation																																							
Paralysis																																							
Palsy																																							
Scrofula																																							
Suicide																																							
Scurvy																																							
Stillborn																																							
Scalded																																							
Teething																																							
Throat, disease of																																							
Violence																																							
Cause not known																																							
TOTAL																																							

CRIME.

CHARGES of MISDEMEANORS before the POLICE COURTS in WESTERN AUSTRALIA during 1859, against the FREE POPULATION and TICKET-OF-LEAVE MEN.

CRIME.	PERTH.						FREMANTLE.						GUILDFORD.						YORK.						TOODYAY.						BUNBURY.						VASSE.						ALBANY.						VICTORIA.						TOTAL.					
	Free.	Expiree.	Conditional Pardon Men.	Ticket-of-Leave Men.	Females.	Total.	Free.	Expiree.	Conditional Pardon Men.	Ticket-of-Leave Men.	Females.	Total.	Free.	Expiree.	Conditional Pardon Men.	Ticket-of-Leave Men.	Females.	Total.	Free.	Expiree.	Conditional Pardon Men.	Ticket-of-Leave Men.	Females.	Total.	Free.	Expiree.	Conditional Pardon Men.	Ticket-of-Leave Men.	Females.	Total.	Free.	Expiree.	Conditional Pardon Men.	Ticket-of-Leave Men.	Females.	Total.	Free.	Expiree.	Conditional Pardon Men.	Ticket-of-Leave Men.	Females.	Total.	Free.	Expiree.	Conditional Pardon Men.	Ticket-of-Leave Men.	Females.	Total.	Free.	Expiree.	Conditional Pardon Men.	Ticket-of-Leave Men.	Females.	Total.	Free.	Expiree.	Conditional Pardon Men.	Ticket-of-Leave Men.	Females.	Total.

Or as opposite.

WESTERN AUSTRALIA.

REPORT

ON THE

GENERAL STATISTICS OF THE COLONY,

FOR THE YEAR

1859,

BY

ALFRED DURLACHER,

REGISTRAR GENERAL.

Printed by Authority at the Government Press.

ERRATA.

1st Page.

4th paragraph, 4th line for " 40 per cent." *read* " 45,"
Do.   do.   for " £56,214"   *read* " £55,792."
Do.   do   for " 155 per cent." *read* " 156."
6th paragraph, 1st line for " £13,769"   *read* " £13,871."
Do.   2nd line for " £10,676"   *read* " £ 9613."
Do.   do.   for " £24,345"   *read* " £23,481."

REPORT

ON THE CONDITION OF THE COLONY OF

WESTERN AUSTRALIA,

AS SHEWN BY THE CENSUS TAKEN

On the 31st December, 1859.

BY ALFRED DURLACHER, REGISTRAR GENERAL

In reporting on the Statistics of the Colony of Western Australia for the Year 1859, I am happy in being enabled to state that a marked prosperity attaches to every Interest therein.

The Farmer finds a steady and remunerative market for his produce—the Grazier for his stock, and the Merchant and Trader equally prosper in increased business. Exports have greatly increased, and the balance of Trade is largely in favor of the Colony.

This is the first Report I have made in which I can state that all despondency has disappeared as to the prospects of the Colony, as up to this time there were always those who took a gloomy view of those prospects, but which gloom has been dispelled by unmistakeable advance, and those who had acquired a habit of viewing despondingly every thing relating to Western Australia, are now obliged to be silent on that point, or admit a change of opinion.

As compared with 1854, the year when the last Census was taken, the increase of the Population has been 3094, or 26·34 per cent., that of Males 1743 or 22·40 per cent., and of Females 1351 or 34·08 per cent. The increase of the Colonial Revenue has been £14,593, or nearly 40 per cent.; of Exports £56,214 or 155 per cent., at the same time that the Imperial Expenditure has decreased £40,525, or about 30 per cent., while the Colonial Debt has been reduced from £12,939 in 1855 to £1750, in 1859.

Since 1854 but four Settlers with Capital arrived in the Colony, yet the number of Agricultural laborers has increased by 1069—the number of Farmers who employ laborers has increased 87—and the increase in the number of Farmers who do not employ labor has been 110.

The increase of Cultivated lands has been 13,769 acres; of lands Fallowed and Cleared ready for Cultivation 10,076—in all 24,845 acres.

The Mercantile Interest is also in a very healthy state.

In 1854 the Average Weekly Amount of Liabilities of the Western Australian Bank was £49000, of Assets £60274; in 1859 these were £61000, and £74659, shewing an increase in Assets of £14425 or 22 per cent. and of Liabilities of £12000, or 24·5 per cent.

And whereas in 1854 the Exports and Imperial Expenditure or money brought into the Colony exceeded the Imports or money taken out of the Colony by £40582, in 1859—the former exceeded the latter by £59,216; although the Imperial Expenditure in 1859 was £40,525 less than in 1854.

POPULATION.

On the 31st December 1859, the Total Population was 14,837, of whom 9522 were Males and 5315 were Females.

Under 15 years of age there were 2410 males and 2444 females or 4854 in all—of 15 years of age and upwards there were 9983 of whom 7112 were males and 2871 were females : there were 2698 married men and 2070 married women ; 4414 single adult* men to 801 single adult women.

THE PROPORTIONS OF THE ABOVE WERE AS FOLLOW :—

	TOTAL POPULATION.		ADULT.			MARRIED.			ADULT, SINGLE.		
	Males	Females	Males	Females	Total	Males	Females	Total	Males	Females	Total
In each 100 of whole Population ..	64·17	35·83	47·93	19·35	67·28	18·19	13·96	32·15	29·75	5·39	35·14
In each 100 of Males.............	..	..	74·69	..	..	23·34	..	..	46·35	..	..
In each 100 of Females.............	..	..	..	54·01	..	.,	38·95	..	..	15·06	..
In each 100 of Adult Males........	..	..	..	..	..	37·93	..	..	62·07	..	..
In each 100 of Adult Females......	..	..	..	..	..	..	72 1	..	..	27·9	..

The total increase of the population since 1854 has been 3094 or 26·34 per cent., being an Annual Average increase of 5·27 per cent. ; of this 1743 were males, and 1351 females, the increase of the former being 22·40 per cent., of the latter 34·08 per cent.

The increase of Adult males has been 964 or 15·63 per cent. ; and of Adult females 674 or 30·65 per cent ; the total Adult increase being 1638, or 19·63 per cent.

The increase in the various Districts, (including Military, Prisoners, and 50 Ticket-of-Leave Men on the hands of Government, 29 of whom were in Hospital, and 21 in Depôt) has been—

DISTRICT.	MALES.	FEMALES.	TOTAL.	INCREASE MALES PER CENT.	INCREASE FEMALES PER CENT.	TOTAL INCREASE PER CENT.
Fremantle	61	105	166	3·34	10·76	6·07
Murray	71	44	115	44·09	44·	44·06
Perth	375	239	614	23·47	20·90	22·46
Sussex...................	206	100	306	98·56	102·04	96·67
Swan	66	62	128	8·07	15·19	11·45
Toodyay	286	249	535	35·56	99· 6	51·06
Victoria	399	183	582	142·5	250·68	164·87
Wellington	35	94	129	5·6	33·21	14·32
York	337	280	617	40·38	76·01	51·53
	1836	1356	3192			
Deduct decrease in Plantagenet	93	5	98			
Total increase....	1743	1351	3094	22·40	34·08	26·34

*By adult is meant of 15 years of age and upwards.

On 31st December, 1859, there were 2010 married men living with their wives, and 688 whose wives were not in the Colony, or 2698 married men in all ; 2010 married women living with their husbands, and 60 whose husbands were not in the Colony, or 2070 married women in all.

There were 4414 single adult men and 801 single adult women : deducting from these, monks, nuns, and others too old to marry there were 4297 marriageable single men to 747 marriageable single women, or 100 males to about 18 women, or 100 women to about 576 males. Add to these the 638 married men whose wives were not in the Colony ; there were 4935 males to 747 females or 100 males to about 15 females, or 100 females to about 662 males, and this last is the proportion of the sexes to be dealt with.

The last calculation gives the following District return :—

District.	More Single Adult Males than Females.	100 Men to about Females.
Albany	331	8
Fremantle	771	16
Murray	86	23
Perth	668	20
Sussex	230	12
Swan	433	13
Toodyay	577	8
Victoria	597	5
Wellington	241	20
York	514	15
	4251	
Deduct excess of non-marriageable single males over non-marriageable single females	63	
Total excess of males	4188	15

Of the 7112 Adult Males there were on 31st December, 1859—

	Married Men Living with their Wives.	Married Men whose Wives were Absent.	Total Married Men.	Single Men.	Total Adult Males.
Free Civilians	1594	36	1630	1467	3097
*Military	96	..	96	73	169
Total who arrived in the Colony as free men, or who was born therein	1690	36	1726	1540	3266
Expirees and Conditional Pardon Men	246	154	400	773	1173
Ticket-of-Leave Men	64	174	238	1428	1666
Prisoners	10	324	334	673	1007
Total who arrived in the Colony as Prisoners or Ticket-of-Leave Men	320	652	972	2874	3846

* By Military is meant the Companies of the 12th Regiment and Royal Engineers, the Pensioners being permanently resident are included in the General Population.

Thus the number of Free marriageable men, without taking into consideration the Bond Population was more than double of the whole of the marriageable females in the Colony.

Distinguishing these classes into Free and Bond, there were 754 more free married male adults than married bond, and 1334 more single bond than free male adults; and in all 580 more bond than free male adults, which latter is shewn by the following District return :—

In Fremantle there were 157 more Bond than Free male adults. In Perth 36, in Sussex 30, Swan 84, Toodyay 94, Victoria 132, Wellington 4, York 157, there being in Plantagenet 76 more Free Male Adults than Bond, and in Murray 58 more Free Male Adults than Bond.

THE AGES OF THE POPULATION WERE AS FOLLOWS :—

	MALES.	FEMALES.	TOTAL
Under 1	263	313	567
„ 5	1125	1155	2280
„ 15	2410	2444	4854
Under 21	2973	3068	6011
21 and upwards	6549	2247	8796
80 and upwards	2	2	4
70 do.	26	17	43
60 do.	164	69	233
50 do.	716	216	932
40 do.	1825	595	1420
30 do.	4197	1239	5436

Not including Military, Prisoners, or Ticket-of-Leave Men in Depôt, the ages of married and single were—

			MALES.	FEMALES.	TOTAL.
Above 15 and Under 21.	Married	....	2	113	115
	Single	....	557	495	1052
Above 15 and Under 40.	Married	....	1246	1429	2675
	Single	....	2960	756	3716
Above 40.	Married	....	1011	545	1556
	Single	....	669	45	714

As classed under Free and Bond, the ages, including all classes, were :—

MALES.	15 TO 21	21 TO 30	30 TO 40	40 TO 50	50 TO 60	60 AND UPWARDS.
Free.	508	787	922	484	360	91
Bond.	5	1497	1450	629	192	73

The principal fact calling for attention in the foregoing statistics is the disproportion of the sexes, and in stating that there are 4297 marriageable men including Prisoners, or 3290 men not including them, to 747 marriageable women, we must in the first place consider one very important point, and that is, there are nearly 400 single Immigrant girls in the Colony, very few of whom would object to marry a respectable man whether of one class or the other, who might be enabled to keep a wife in some degree of comfort.

The question therefore arises, how is it, if there be so many of these men who wish to marry that such a number of Immigrant women are still single.

I must here admit that I have always viewed the disproportion of the sexes with great alarm, and now that I have the results of the Census of 1859 before me; although much of that alarm appears to me to have been groundless, still the disproportion is much greater than desirable, and had Convicts arrived at the rate they were expected, namely 1000 a year, had not female immigration proportionably increased, great and serious evils must have resulted; as the mere immigration of the number of single women who could have been absorbed in private service would not have preserved anything like a due proportion of the sexes.

And even as things are at present, how an Immigration of single women is to be carried out so as to reduce the existing disproportion of males is a subject of great perplexity, as if Free Female Immigrants be not confined to the number who could find employment in private service, which at present at the most is not more than 250 in the year, it entails the necessity of keeping up Depôts of unemployed girls, the evil of which is that it engenders in them habits of idleness; and idleness and temptation might induce many to wander from the paths of rectitude.

I know not of any employment for them in Depôt, and there is no power to prevent them leaving it when they please, even had the Authorities the knowledge that they left it to enter a life of immorality—the women are Free Immigrants, and they cannot be made Prisoners.

I speak from many years experience as Immigration Officer, when I state that it is most injurious to Female Immigrants to be any length of time idling in the Government Depôts— wandering about the Town on afternoons, exposed to temptation from those (and there are many such) who would lead them astray; and moreover they form acquaintances in the town —the remembrance of whom makes many of them discontented with Country life, and even with the discipline those who leave their places in the Country and return to Depôt are subjected to, many still do so—but they are only those who have been left a sufficient length of time in Depôt to have acquired a liking for Town life, and a desire to imitate the ridiculous display in dress, so conspicuous in the servant girls in Perth and Fremantle.

The question to be solved is how to increase the Female Immigration to the Colony to the benefit of the Immigrants and the Colony at large,—a question I admit I am quite unable to answer satisfactorily although it is my opinion that the injury inflicted on the morality of the community by the introduction of a larger number of Females than could be readily employed in Private service however objectionable it may be, is very preferable to the crime engendered by the association of a number of Men together without a due proportion of Females

RELIGIOUS DENOMINATIONS.

The Religious Denominations on 31st December, 1859 were, Church of England, 9942; Wesleyans, 835; Independents, 385; other Protestants, 270; total Protestants, 11432; Church of Rome, 3354; Jews, Mahometans and Pagans, 51; of these there were :—

	Church of England	Wesleyans	Independents	Other Protestants	Total Protestants	Church of Rome	Jews, Mahometans Pagans
General Population	9030	827	257	270	10384	2875	47
Military	232	8	128	..	368	106	..
Prisoners and Ticket-of Leave Men in Depot	680	..	..	..	680	373	4

As compared with the year 1854, not including Prisoners or Ticket-of-Leave Men in Depôt, there were :—

	CHURCH OF ENGLAND.	WESLEYANS.	OTHER PROTESTANTS.	TOTAL PROTESTANTS.	CHURCH OF ROME
1859	9262	835	655	10752	2981
1854	6656	580	793	8038	2034
Increase	2606	246	....	2714	·947
Increase per cent. ..	39·12	41·76	....	33·76	46·55
Decrease	....	....	138	....	....
Decrease per cent. ..	....	....	17·14	....	....

The following Table shews the per centage of the Religious Denominations in the Colony :—

	CHURCH OF ENGLAND.			WESLEYANS.			OTHER PROTESTANTS.			TOTAL PROTESTANTS.			CHURCH OF ROME.		
	Males	Females	Total	Males	Females	Total	Males	Females	Total	Males	Females	Total	Males	Females	Total
	6541	3401	9042	455	580	835	389	266	655	7855	4047	11432	2100	1254	3354
Of each Church	65·79	94·21	...	54·5	45·4	...	59·39	40·61	...	64·6	35·4	...	62·61	37·39	...
Of Male Population	66·69	...	...	4·78	...	...	4·19	...	...	77·50	...	...	22·05	...	...
Of Female Population	...	63·98	...	...	7·14	...	...	5·04	...	...	76·13	...	...	23·09	...
Of Total Population............	...	...	67	...	...	5·65	...	...	4·42	...	...	77·05	...	...	22·6

And there are also 47 Jews, Mahometans and Pagans—viz. 33 males and 14 females.

With regard to the number of Protestants, although they can be depended on in the aggregate, they cannot be entirely under their distinctive heads, as many Presbyterians and other Dissenters not having their own Ministers here, attend other Protestant Churches in which they are therefore classed.

There are in the Colony eleven Ministers of the Church of England performing parochial duties, 2 Wesleyan Ministers, 2 Independent Ministers, and 15 of the Church of Rome, and although this gives but an average charge of 904 persons to each Church of England Minister, 418 to each Wesleyan, 193 to each Independent, and 224 to each Minister of the Church of Rome; it must be borne in mind that the persons forming these Congregations are scattered over a Country of about 600 miles in length by about 100 in breadth.

The total Church accommodation for the Members of the Church of England is about 3000 sittings for nearly 10,000 persons, for the Wesleyans and other Protestants about 900, for about 1500 people, and for the Roman Catholics, about 800 for about 3500 people.

COUNTRY OF BIRTH.

The following Table shews the Country of Birth of the Population not including Military and their families, Prisoners and Ticket-of-Leave Men in Depot.

	ENGLAND	IRELAND	SCOTLAND	WALES	OTHER BRITISH POSSESSIONS	WESTERN AUSTRALIA	FOREIGNERS.
Males........	3830	1304	367	58	98	2335	171
Females	1818	1102	111	17	87	2279	20
Total.	5348	2406	487	75	185	4614	191

Of the whole Male Population of 9522, on 31st December, 1859, 2335, or about 24 per cent. were born in the Colony, 293 or about 3 per cent. arrived as Military and their sons; 3048, or about 32 per cent. arrived as Free Immigrants; and 3846 or about 41 per cent. were sent here as Convicts, and of the whole Female Population 2279, or 43 per cent. were born in the Colony, and 3036 or 57 per cent. were Immigrants.

OCCUPATIONS.

The occupations of the male population on 31st December, 1859, were:—Farming and Grazing, 3066; Trade, 378, Mechanics, Artizans, &c. 867; Medical Profession 12; Legal Profession 3; Clergymen 32; Government Civil Service 235; Laborers, not Agricultural 1016; Male Domestic Servants 207; Seamen 76; Gardeners 47; Schoolmasters 20; Veterinary Surgeons 2, and No Occupation, 10; Military 169; Prisoners 1007, and Ticket-of-Leave Men in Depôt 21, and in Hospital 29.

There were also 356 Female domestic servants.

The increase on 1854 has been—

Agriculture and Grazing,	1307,	or about	75	per cent.
Trade and Commerce,	196,	or ,,	106	do.
Mechanics, Artizans, &c.,	363,	or ,,	72	do.
Laborers, not Agricultural, and Male Domestic Servants, ...	247,	or ,,	25	do.
Female Domestic Servants	104,	or ,,	42	do.

Since 1854, 1338 Free Male Adult Immigrants have arrived in the Colony, and the Emigration of Adult Males, Free, Expirees and Conditional Pardon Men has been 1874, making an excess of Emigration of 536 Free Male Adults.

The following Table shews the Immigration and Emigration from the Colony since 1854:—

ADULT FREE IMMIGRATION AND EMIGRATION (THE LATTER INCLUDING EXPIREES AND CONDITIONAL PARDON MEN.)

	Immigration.			Emigration.			Excess of Immigration.			Excess of Emigration.		
	M	F	Total.	M	F	Total.	M	F	Total.	M	F	Total.
1855	416	279	695	468	136	604	..	143	143	52	..	52
1856	191	139	330	354	141	495	..	..	..	163	2	165
1857	233	195	428	587	195	782	..	..	..	354	.	354
1858	251	234	485	346	128	474	..	106	106	95	..	95
1859	247	364	611	119	53	172	128	311	439	..	..	..
	1338	1211	2549	1874	653	2527	128	560	688	664	2	666

TOTALS FREE ADULTS.

Year.	Excess of Immigration.	Excess of Emigration.
1855	91	..
1856	..	165
1857	..	354
1858	11	..
1859	439	..
	541	519

Increase Females 558
Decrease Males 536

TOTALS OF ALL AGES.

Year.	Excess Immigration.	Excess Emigration.
1855	189	..
1856	..	197
1857	..	412
1858	38	..
1859	517	..

The number of Convicts who have arrived in the Colony since 1854 has been 2368; therefore since the 31st December, 1854 the total excess of Immigration over Emigration has been, Males, 1732, and Females 558.

The total number of Convicts who have arrived in the Colony since it was made a Penal Settlement is about 5000.

It will be here seen that in 1859, the tide of Emigration had comparatively dwindled down to a very small number, and this is a very favourable fact in the progress of Western Australia as shewing the increased demand for labor and greater inducements to remain in the Colony.

That many of the Convicts who have filled respectable situations in life, will leave the Colony so soon as they obtain their Conditional Pardons is to be expected, as they naturally would wish to leave a place where the fact of their having been Convicts is patent to all, for other spots where their former delinquencies might not be known.

EDUCATION.

Exclusive of Military, Prisoners and Ticket-of-Leave Men in Depôt, of the 11,134 persons of 5 years of age and upwards in the Colony on 31st December, 1859, (viz. 7113 males and 4021 females) 6946 or 62·5 per cent. could read and write; 1176 or 10·4 per cent. could read only, and 8122 or 72·95 per cent. could read; thus 4188 or 37·61 per cent could not write; and 3012 or 27·05 per cent. could neither read nor write.

Of the 7113 males above 5 years of age and upwards, 4651 or 65·39 per cent. could read and write, 637 or 8·95 per cent. could read only, and 5288 or 74·35 per cent. could read; thus 2462 or 34·61 per cent. could not write, and 1825 or 25·65 could neither read nor write.

Of the 4021 females above 5 years of age, 2295 or 57·09 per cent. could read and write, 539 or 13·4 per cent. could read only, and 2834 or 70·5 per cent. could read; thus 1726 or 42·91 per cent. could not write, and 1187 or 29·5 per cent. neither read or write.

Thus out of every 100 there were about—

	Who could read and write.	Who could read only.	Who could read.	Who could not write.	Who could neither read nor write.
Males	65	9	74	35	26
Females.........	57	14	71	43	29

ABORIGINES.

But little that is satisfactory can be said with regard to the Natives—they are gradually disappearing before the advance of the White man, their Civilization taking too much the form of acquiring many of the European's bad habits and but few of his good ones—they learn to drink and smoke, and Immorality in their Women has now become an habitual custom, regarded as a matter of course by their husbands and parents. Many philanthropic attempts have been made, and much money expended in attempting to reclaim these people, but with the two exceptional cases of the few children with the Sisters of Mercy at Perth, and those under the care of Mrs. Camfield at Albany, they have all failed.

In 1842 the number of Aborigines frequenting the Settled Districts of Perth, Fremantle, Swan, Avon, Wellington, Sussex and Albany was estimated at about 1200, whereas at the present time they are not supposed to exceed 800, and this mainly arises from the gross immorality of the women preventing their bearing children; there may be, and doubtless are many other causes, but this is the chief one.

It may be asked, is it not possible to reclaim these people—my experience among them for many years in nearly every part of the Colony tells me it is not, unless taken as Children before they have acquired a love for their wild free life; and from the objection of the parents generally to give up their children to the White Man, but little good can be done in that way—and even of those who had been brought up in this manner by the Wesleyan Mission from 1840 to 1845, but very few have not taken to their former uncivilized state, the same as if they had never known better things.

Many of the Aborigines are civilized to the extent of becoming servants to the White Men so long as it suits their tastes, but very few of these remain permanently under restraint, but twice in the year generally return to their Bush Friends and Savage Life, I suppose as a kind of holiday, when they need not acknowledge any master—but this class have acquired too great a liking for bread to be long away from the means of obtaining it, and I believe that those who do frequent the White Man's dwellings do so merely for the purpose of gratifying their appetites, and not from any conviction of the superiority of the European in any other way than in the power of raising and obtaining food.

But 176 Males and 69 Females of the Aboriginal tribes are returned as in the permanent employ of the settlers, and of these 31 men and 12 women are attached to the Roman Catholic Mission in the Victoria Plains; 4 boys and 14 girls are in the Institution at Albany, leaving but 141 Men and 43 Women actually employed by the settlers.

IMPERIAL EXPENDITURE.

The Imperial Expenditure in 1859 was £92,070; £34,007 being for Military Services including Amount drawn by Staff Officer of Pensioners for Pensioners, and £58063 for Civil Services; this is a reduction of £40,525 on 1854, arising from the completion of Imperial Buildings, and the reduced price of provisions.

The total Expenditure under this head since the introduction of Convicts in 1850, has been—

	1850	1851	1852	1853	1854	1855	1856	1857	1858	1859
	£	£	£	£	£	£	£	£	£	£
Military	10760	15276	39961	42107	53124	35286	31645	34126	48629	34007
Convict	4497	34103	45024	52665	76537	77374	61645	57196	51981	53871
Other Civil Services	6896	6960	7372	8230	2936	2037	187	..	7435	4194
Total ..	22153	56339	92357	103002	132597	114697	93477	91322	108045	92072

Thus nearly One Million of Money has been expended in the Colony from Imperial Funds since Western Australia was made a Penal Settlement.

In 1859 there were 2200 of all occupations who were engaged on their own account, and not in employ as servants, laborers, &c.; among these the Imperial Expenditure was nearly £42 per head; of this Expenditure of £90,6061, about £450000 has been paid for pay and allowances, including the amount received by Pensioners, about £250000 for provisions produced in the Colony; and £206000 for imported provisions and stores.

I may here state to shew what the introduction of Convicts has done for the Colony, that—

THE TOTAL AMOUNT OF	For the 21 years previously to their introduction—that is from 1829 to 1849 inclusive.	For the 10 years since their introduction—that is from 1850 to 1859 inclusive.
The Imperial Expenditure was....	£ 375,264	£ 905,971
,, Colonial Revenue was	123,813	340,753
,, Exports	175,843	463,184
The Tonnage of Ships arriving ...	Tons..223,758	Tons ..374,432
No. of Acres cultivated	Acres..61,442	Acres .. 137,108

GIVING AN ANNUAL AVERAGE

	PREVIOUS TO THE INTRODUCTION OF CONVICTS.	SINCE THE INTRODUCTION OF CONVICTS.	INCREASE PER CENT.
Of Imperial Expenditure..	£ 17,870	£ 90,597	407
,, Colonial Revenue	5,896	34,075	480
,, Exports	8,374	46,318	453
The tonnage of Ships arriving	Tons ..10,655	Tons..37,443	251
,, No. of Acres cultivated	Acres .. 2926	13,711	368

COLONIAL REVENUE.

The Colonial Revenue in 1859, was £48,754, being an increase of £14,573, or 42·6 per cent. on that for 1854.

The increase in Customs has been £6608 or 29·75 per cent. ; on Land Revenue, £5012, or 85·67 per cent. ; on Harbor Duties, £800, or 172·78 per cent. ; on Licenses for Public Houses, &c., £1090 or 75·53 per cent. ; on Postage, £1110 or 77·29 per cent.

Colonial Revenue.

	1854	1855	1856	1857	1858	1859
CUSTOMS—Duty on Spirits ..	12416	10582	14219	8161	11135	13492
Wine ..	1030	641	840	288	668	523
Beer ..	49	314	653	732	2071	1171
TOTAL ON SPIRITS, WINE, AND BEER....	13495	11537	15712	9181	13874	15186
Tobacco	2387	2637	4226	1940	4371	4884
AD VALOREM ..	5246	3831	4566	3656	5492	4650
Tea ..	201	953	1103	567	971	1152
Coffee	24	52	54	30	48	76
Sugar	523	1469	498	1358	1514	2413
Warehouse Rent, &c.	358	309	433	233	595	470
Kangaroo Skins, &c.	11	152	14	21	96	22
Total Customs...............	22245	20940	26606	16986	26961	28853
LAND SALES ..	2759	3925	3484	2199	4384	4165
,, Rent	55	..	..	10	15	43
Depasturing Licenses and Leases	2813	3017	3420	3687	4101	4721
Tillage Leases	45	114	228	302	604	712
Timber Licenses	72	131	92	202	257	360
Rottnest .	..	70	..	430	652	733
Transfer Duties..	106	88	124	130	83	128
Total Land	5850	7345	7348	6960	10096	10862

Colonial Revenue,—*continued.*

	1854	1855	1856	1857	1858	1859
Harbor Dues	463	609	766	702	973	1263
Auction Duties	254	342	372	401	254	429
Licenses	1120	1272	1371	2136	2144	2190
Postages	1436	1151	2102	1842	2147	2546
Judicial Fines and Fees	744	720	971	822	772	937
Fees of Office	463	499	553	435	384	381
Sale of Government Property	267	393	630	298	228	127
Miscellaneous and Special	740	202	156	193	43	125
Refunds	..	204	455	136	318	246
Reimbursements	450	667	665	625	613	674
Rents exclusive of Land	129	108	108	97	106	121
	6066	6167	8149	7687	7982	9039
TOTAL	34161	34452	42103	31633	45039	48754
Imperial Aid	7523	9087	8125	7375	7764	9191
Grand Total	41684	43559	50228	39008	52803	57945
Loan from W. Australian Bank	1823	5110	943	1916		

On taking a review of the Customs Revenue for the last 10 years, commencing from the year 1850, when the Convicts were first introduced, it will be seen that there has been a steady progression from £7803 in that year to £28,853 in 1859 : but there are some peculiarities appearing on the face of these tabular returns which require notice and explanation.

The greatest increase appears to have been made in the Revenue of the first five years ending 1854, when it reached the sum of £22,245, and this is mainly attributable to the impetus given to the general Trade and Commerce of the Colony by the aid of Convict labor, and a large Imperial Expenditure, and the reaction which took place on the possession of these advantages from a state of despondency to one of energy and hope naturally led to speculations and somewhat excessive importations which had obtained their culminating point in 1854—for a considerable reduction took place in the succeeding year, and that in the face of specific duties on Beer, Tea, Sugar and Coffee. The next striking peculiarity is the difference of Revenue between the years 1856 and 1857, there being a falling off of nearly £10,000 in the latter year. During that year many circumstances had tended to cast a gloom over the prospects of the Colony, especially the doubt and uncertainty of the duration of the Convict system, and a depressing effect was produced on the general prosperity. But the principal cause of the difference, arose from the alteration of the scale of Import duties in July 1856, on which occasion, holders of Spirits, Wines and Tobacco were permitted to pay duties at the old rate, thus increasing the Revenue of 1856, to the prejudice of the next year, the effect of which may be appreciated by comparing the receipts of the two years, viz., Spirits, £14,219 and £8161 ; Wine, £840, and £288 ; Tobacco, £4226 and £1940.

With reference to the consumption of the several articles which may be distinguished under the head of luxuries in contradistinction from necessaries, the principal items of which are Spirits, Wines, Beer and Tobacco, it may be observed that although the general population has increased from 11,743 in 1854, when the former Census was taken, to 14,837 in 1859, the consumption of these articles has not kept pace with the increase of population as the duties of 1859—although considerably in advance of 1854—do not indicate a larger quantity consumed, due allowance being made for the increased rate of duties, therefore the rate of consumption has been reduced in proportion to the increase, and the reason of this is palpably from the use of Colonial Wine and Beer, which has been produced in large quantities and as will no doubt, with improvement in manufacture, become gradually more in favor and be substituted in a great measure for Spirits and Foreign Wine.

COLONIAL EXPENDITURE.

The Colonial Expenditure for 1859 was £45,727, being an increase of £24,56 on 1854.

SERVICE.	1854	1855	1856	1857	1858	1859
	£	£	£	£	£	£
Governor	2070	1640	429	274	273	278
Colonial Secretary	2066	2185	2114	2126	2058	2178
Councils	374	362	475	264	222	218
Treasurer and Auditor	1093	1288	1280	1280	1280	1280
Registry	100	100	100	100	100	100
Survey Department	3789	2828	2233	2244	2310	2347
Public Works	7628	7366	5002	5287	4075	7404
Customs and Revenue	1118	1172	1178	1725	1822	1889
Post Office	2053	2046	2210	2335	2225	2494
Harbor Master	1250	1528	1901	1794	1947	1986
Judicial	2767	5228	5252	4633	5322	5715
Ecclesiastical	1489	1966	1681	1722	1662	2186
Medical	1457	1673	1654	1795	1681	1943
Police	9382	9169	7982	9520	10759	11715
Gaols	3010	3614	2132	1724	1042	1223
Aborigines	1708	1119	1010	945	1040	1209
Commandant	185	61	..	..	..	..
Education	911	1339	1065	1451	1396	1565
Immigration	830	819	510	436	396	571
Pensions, &c.	54	26	51	230	404	462
Charitable Allowances	342	294	380	817	698	918
Rent	229	361	327	341	285	262
Miscellaneous	560	1278	530	1645	1547	5617
Repayment of Debts, Interest, &c.	..	1652	6041	919	3375	105
Rottnest	..	..	1331	942	907	1198
Refunds	..	156	32	433	200	55
Total £	44383	49240	46990	44992	47119	54918
Total Establishments	25558	28355	25897	27773	29041	29851
Exclusive of ditto	18825	20885	21093	17219	18078	25067
Total as above £	44383	49240	46990	44992	47119	54918
Total Colonial	36860	40153	38865	37617	39355	45727
Imperial Aid	7523	9087	8125	7375	7764	9191
Total as above £	44383	49240	46990	44992	47119	54918

GOVERNOR'S OFFICE.—In 1854 the Expenditure was £2070, and in 1859 £278. This difference arises from the Governor's own salary of £1800 per annum being drawn in England and not therefore appearing as a charge in the books of the Treasurer from which these Returns have been compiled.

MISCELLANEOUS.—The large sum of £5617 in 1859 arises from the sum of £4000 remitted to the Agent General for Current Services, and not classified, and the sum of £1151 on account of Subsidy for Royal Mail Service.

REPAYMENT OF DEBTS.—At the close of 1854 the Debts of the Colony stood as follows— in round numbers.

Due to the Commissariat Department................£3098
    ,,   Imperial Government 2168
    ,,   Agent General 2500
    ,,   Western Australian Bank................ 3000
    ,,   Debentures Outstanding 1124

Amounting altogether to.......................£11888

Since which date, the two first items have been remitted by the Imperial Government, and the debt due to the Agent General has been defrayed from the Imperial Treasury, and the Items which appear under this head of Payment of Debts since 1854 are for payments of Debentures, or Loans outstanding due to the Western Australian Bank ; so that the old Debts of the Local Government have all been either remitted or paid, and the only amount which now comes under this head is the sum of £1750 due on Debentures recently issued on account of Land surrendered for Episcopal purposes and bearing Interest at 6 per cent.

IMPORTS.

The value of Imports for 1859 amounted to £125,315, shewing a decrease on 1854 of £2945, made up of £1758 on Clothing ; £1311 Cabinet Ware and Upholstery ; of £4417 on Spirituous and Fermented Liquors, and £22427 on Miscellaneous articles, against an increase of £19459 on Tea and Sugar, of £521 on Tobacco ; £2790 on Hardware and Cutlery ; £1099 on Machinery, and £3099 on Miscellaneous Articles.

TABLE of IMPORTS from 1854 to 1859 inclusive.

	1854	1855	1856	1857	1858	1859
	£	£	£	£	£	£
ARTICLES OF FOOD,— Butter and Cheese	2647	1537	3279	1804	2169	2734
Corn	2299	1246	557	160	1844	1272
Coffee	314	530	561	305	575	693
Fruits, dried	1173	820	839	1610	1121	899
Flour, Meal and Bread	12604	6990	7595	3814	7990	3490
Hops	1251	513	675	327	423	192
Meats, Salted and Preserved	3430	3026	3989	1539	1821	1492
Oilman's Stores	6657	3598	5624	3839	5592	4512
Rice	2220	1773	675	1054	1758	830
Sugar	7093	10947	3158	10944	14981	20899
Tea	1733	5091	6036	3593	5792	7486
Total articles of Food	40821	36071	32983	28389	43476	44409
TOBACCO,— Manufactured	2100	2908	3715	921	2195	2138
Unmanufactured	122	78	177	269	247	158
Cigars	313	338	417	383	333	737
Snuff	8	30		21	51	31
Total Tobacco	2543	3354	4309	1594	2826	3064
SPIRITS, WINE, BEER, &c. Brandy	4440	5536	7579	4740	2592	3907
Geneva	359	77	74	66	173	93
Gin	717	520	1192	982	1230	873
Rum	1325	920	1536	1130	1620	646
Whiskey				9	7	8
Liquors	44	27	5	41	91	4
Total Spirits	6885	7080	10586	6968	5713	5531
Wine	2860	1713	2641	1036	4297	1735
BEER AND CIDER, BOTTLED.	4224	1601	2734	1356	4843	1572
Beer and Cider, draught	4399	1893	2656	2844	8628	4813
Total Beer and Cider	8623	3494	5390	4200	13471	6385
Total, Wine, Spirits and Beer	18368	12287	18417	12204	23481	13951

Imports—*continued.*

ARTICLES OF CLOTHING.	1854	1855	1856	1857	1858	1859
	£	£	£	£	£	£
Apparel and slops	6747	5357	6553	5922	6857	9040
Boots and Shoes	4449	2326	3459	2714	3885	3067
Drapery, Millinery, &c.	26064	21180	23525	17857	26846	23572
Hats and Bonnets	1196	1449	686	1063	959	1019
Total Clothing	38456	30312	34203	27556	38547	36698
Animals	75	130	223	175	405	300
Apothecaries wares	915	257	461	710	1243	933
Brooms	354	447	153	119	80	106
Bags and Sacks	401	623	1060	1533	2030	535
Books and Stationery	2208	1289	2786	1071	2212	2178
Cordage ..	1100	2365	1232	1153	1527	1154
Cabinet Ware and Upholstery	2568	1635	3029	1128	1817	1257
Carts and Carriages	500	103	510	327	323	278
Deals and Timber	755	1246	914	670	1023	352
Earthenware and Glass	1731	1180	1950	1330	1898	1059
Hardware and Cutlery	1212	1449	2171	1734	3060	4002
Iron and Ironware ..	3598	5353	5464	4421	7001	4813
Leather	1886	171	665	298	654	432
Lead	590	48	8	654	923	..
Machinery	..	..	..	2982	2416	1099
Mats and Baskets ..	72	125	66	101	185	243
Oils, Colors, &c.	825	398	289	168	934	208
Powder and Shot	511	311	973	319	402	978
Saddlery and Harness	1894	789	826	837	1316	1124
Soap and Candles ..	3423	1869	2939	2289	4267	3047
Tools and Implements	1776	2249	5620	179	256	136
Wood Goods	76	218	210	103	505	801
All other articles	1602	1041	1472	2488	2125	2158
	28072	23296	33021	24789	36602	27193
TOTAL IMPORTS	128260	105320	122938	49532	144932	125815

Taking the Imported quantities at the average market prices, the following amounts have been expended on Tobacco, Spirits and Fermented liquors during the last ten years :—

ON TOBACCO.	1850 to 1859 inclusive.	Yearly Average.
Manufactured		
Unmanufactured	58860	5886
Cigars		
Snuff		
On Spirits	308800	30880
,, Wine	44860	4486
,, Beer	184600	18460
Total Wine Spirits and Beer	558260	55826

ON ARTICLES OF CLOTHING.

£614,740, or a yearly average of £61,474

Taking the average of 1858 and 1859, the following consumption appears as Imported

SPIRITS	WINE	BEER AND CIDER	TOTAL
Gallons.. 21069	6552	96860	1244471

Taking the consumption of Spirituous Liquors to be by the whole of the Men above 21 and one-fifth of the women above 21, and the average consumption thereof by one man, at as much as three women, we have as consumers—

6549 Men
450 Women equal to 150 Men
_____
6699   Total consumers

Say — 6700
Deduct an average of   1000 Prisoners
_____
Gives   5700

And this would give nearly 30 pints of spirits per annum to each consumer, or about 23 bottles ; and supposing there are 2000 drinkers of Wine, would give also about 26 pints to each, and if there be 5000 Beer drinkers they would have consumed about 153 pints each in the year. Averaging these numbers would give to each person about 210 pints of Spirituous and Fermented liquors, or reducing the whole to the average comparative strength of Beer, would give to each estimated consumer about 400 pints annually ; and this is not taking into consideration the 22000 gallons of Colonial Wine and the quantity of Beer brewed in the Colony, of which latter I cannot form any estimate.

There are several articles of food imported which could well be produced in the Colony.

In 1859 there were imported—

Flour and Biscuit 220 tons, the average retail price of which @ £18 per
    ton gives,... £3960
Butter and Cheese, 54,281 lbs. @ 2s. 4d. lb........................ 5428
Dried Fruits,   8400   „   1s.   „   420
Salt Meats,   116,826   „   1s.   „   5841
                                                £15649

There is however a great reduction in the importation of these articles during the three last years as compared with the three previous ones, thus :—

	1854 TO 1856 INCLUSIVE.	1857 TO 1859 INCLUSIVE.	DECREASE.
	lbs.	lbs.	lbs.
Flour and Biscuit....	3,300,000	2,000,000	1,300,000
Butter and Cheese ..	145,000	134,000	11,000
Dried Fruits........	60,000	53,000	7,000
Salt Meats..........	1,272,000	451,000	821.000

This arises from the increase in Cultivation and Stock thus (the increase of the Population being nearly 27 per cent.)

	1854	1859	INCREASE PER CENT.
Wheat, acres........	5897	13,610	131
Cattle..............	20436	30,999	52
Vineyards, acres	155	363	134
Pigs	4442	11,430	157
Sheep..............	173568	234815	35

And in 1859 there were nearly 520,000 lbs. of Salted Pork, Bacon and Hams, cured in the Colony.

There is a very great increase in the importation of Tea, Coffee and Sugar, thus :—

	1854	1859	AVERAGE TO EACH PERSON 1854.	AVERAGE TO EACH PERSON 1859.
	lbs.	lbs.	lbs.	lbs.
Tea	41,816	138,163	Nearly 3½	Nearly 9½
Sugar.........	1,038,352	1,777,833	87	119¾
Coffee	19,936	41,555	1⅞	2¾

The consumption of Tobacco has not increased in proportion to the Population, thus—

THE IMPORTATIONS HAVE BEEN OF	1854 TO 1856 INCLUSIVE.	1857 TO 1859 INCLUSIVE.	
	lbs.	lbs.	lbs.
Tobacco manufactured	164,000	88,000	Decrease 76,000
Cigars	4,360	4340	Do. 20
Snuff	150	350	Increase 200

This decreased consumption in a great measure arises from the increased price of Tobacco in the three last years, consequent on increased duty and higher cost. Smoking Tobacco in 1854, 1855, and 1856 was retailed here at 2s. 6d. per lb., whereas now the price is from 3s. 9d. to 4s.

There has also been a reduction in the consumption of Rice, arising from the lower price of flour, thus—

	1854 TO 1856 INCLUSIVE	1857 TO 1859 INCLUSIVE.	DECREASE.
Rice imported	910,000 lbs.	762,000 lbs.	148,000 lbs.

The only other Imports necessary to notice are Hardware and Cutlery, and Soap and Candles.

INVOICE VALUE.	1854 TO 1856 INCLUSIVE.	1857 TO 1859 INCLUSIVE.	INCREASE.
Hardware & Cutlery Iron & Ironmongery	£19,247	£30031	10784
Soap and Candles ..	8231	9603	1372

The importation of Soap would have shewn a much greater amount were it not for the increased and increasing consumption of Soap manufactured in the Colony.

THE SHIPPING INWARDS WAS AS FOLLOWS :—

	1854	1859	Increase.	Increase per cent.
Ships 97		111	14	
Tonnage 38963		63414	24451	

EXPORTS.

The increase in the value of Exports is the most satisfactory sign of the progress of the Colony.

The increase in 1859 on 1854 was £56,792, or 156 per cent.

Exports—(Value).

	1854	1855	1856	1857	1858	1859
Animals	50	1786	2060	1782	14035	2750
Butter	..	..	..	..	..	..
Bones	..	..	..	12	..	..
Fish, salted	154	26	4	24	..	..
Hides and Skins....	254	108	128	60	93	9
Hay and Fodder	..	..	..	..	1040	92
Vegetables, Provisions, &c....	215	1544	507	1623	1844	3567
Salt	100	..	78	..	..	..
Tallow	9	..	..	13	..	..
Wool	22341	24724	25672	35886	33969	44600
Flour	..	..	..	168	..	880
Wheat	..	..	..	..	..	16
Wine, Colonial	..	..	..	..	..	106
Horns and Hoofs	..	70	93	..	20	49
Gum	44	..	..	..	224	120
Bricks	75	..	..	..	..	..
Leather....	168	..	..	..	..	180
Lime	30	..	..	..	..	..
Guano	..	125	..	..	..	..
Oil, Whale	591	2530	2926	2520	3474	608
Whale Bone	238	350	533	972	1487	1573
Specimens, Natural History	7	24	..	..	90	45
Sandal Wood	..	..	..	2525	7455	17260
Timber	7023	12077	9671	9449	2340	6331
Wood Work	369	..	18	60	..	..
Lead	2440	2675	1200	2410	1220	495
Copper Ore	..	26	1018	1920	9531	14122
Lead Ore	..	250	..	..	..	135
Wattle Bark	..	..	..	..	42	49
Re-Exports	2137	797	831	534	1785	50
TOTAL..........	36245	47112	44739	59948	78649	93037
Wool exported in lbs.	442881	493073	500996	478486	543504	594665

A great increase appears under the head of Animals; the total for 1854, 1855 and 1856 being £3896, and for the last 3 years £18,567; this arises from the export of Horses to India.

The Values of the Exportations of other articles have been during the last six years—

	1854—1855—1856	1857—1858—1859.
Potatoes and Vegetables ..	£ 2266	£ 6712
Wool	72737	114455
Whalebone	1121	4032
Timber and Sandal Wood	28771	45080
Copper and Lead Ore and Lead	7609	29833
And the Total Exports were ..	127298	231055

The quantity of Wool has not increased in proportion to its value which in 1854, 1855, and 1856 was declared at 1s. per lb., but during the last three years at 1s. 3d. and 1s. 6d. per lb.

The following were the quantities exported :—

1854—1855—1856	1857—1858—1859.
1,437,950 lbs.	1,616,615 lbs.

And the average yield of Wool per fleece has been—

1854	1855	1856	1857	1858	1859
2 lbs. 9 oz.	2 lbs. 6 oz.	2 lbs. 7 oz.	2 lbs. 7 oz.	2 lbs. 8 oz.	2 lbs. 9 oz.

The export of Timber is looked forward to as a great source of wealth to the Colony. We possess an almost inexhaustible supply of the "Jarrah," a timber well suited for railway sleepers, ship building, &c., and a demand already exists for this article in South Australia, Singapore, Ceylon, India and the Mauritius, and but little doubt is entertained, that if once properly introduced into Europe it would be extensively used in Ship Building.

Since 1854 about 7000 tons have been exported.

Sandal Wood is also another very profitable export but if continued to be cut in the quantities sent out of the Colony during the last three years, will gradually be used up.

Since 1856 about 3000 tons of this wood has been sent to Singapore.

There are many other woods indigenous to this Colony that require but to be known to soon come into foreign demand—such as the Tuart, the Blue Gum, &c.

The export of Minerals call for some remarks on the Mining Districts of the Colony, which abound with Mineral indications not only as regards Copper and Lead, but also Gold ; and periodically the excitement of the Public is raised to fever heat by the reports of some new discoveries. The Geological features of several portions of the Territory are so very similar to the Gold producing districts of Victoria, as to render these reports highly probable, and gold has already been found, but not in sufficient quantities to make a workable field of operations.

The Victoria or Champion Bay District not only abounds with indications of the richest description, but valuable lodes of Copper and Lead have been discovered, and several of them have been developed by operations more or less extensive ; an area of 60 or 70 miles square is intersected by an innumerable quantity of Lodes of the richest description of Ore, principally of Copper.

The attention of the public was at a very early period of the Colony's history drawn to this district by the highly favorable report made of it by Sir George (then Lieutenant) Grey, when he passed along the seaboard on his perilous retreat from Shark's Bay, after the wreck of his Boats; and subsequently when he became Governor of South Australia, he stated that after visiting the Mining Districts of that place he felt more and more convinced that the neighbourhood of Champion Bay would eventually turn out to be a very rich Mineral Country. The distance of the place caused it to be unoccupied for some years, and it is only since 1856 that the extent and value of its Mineral Wealth could be in any way appreciated. The discoveries of Mineral lodes have almost invariably been made by Shepherds, and not from any scientific or systematic investigation. The number of these lodes is almost beyond belief, and it would be hazardous to state any opinion of their extent.

CULTIVATION.

The Cultivation in 1859 was 13,610 Acres Wheat ; 4029 Barley ; 617 Oats ; 85 Maize, Beans, &c. ; 5438 Hay and Green Crop ; 574 Kitchen Garden ; 398 Potatoes and Onions ; 363 Vineyard ; 3238 Fallowed, and 8078 cleared for Cultivation ; in all 36430 Acres.

The increase of Cultivation, 1859 on 1854 has been :—

Increase of Wheat,	..	7713 acres or about 131		per cent.
,, Barley,	..	2490	do.	do.	162	,,
,, Oats,	..	282	do.	do.	84	,,
,, Rye,	..	503	do.	do.	246	,,

Increase of Maize and Beans, &c.   24 acres or about 40 per cent
      ,,   Potatoes and Onions, 207 do. do. 94 ,,
      ,,   Hay and Green Crop 2202 do. do. 68 ,,
      ,,   Vineyard ..   208 do. do. 134 ,,
      ,,   Kitchen Garden   232 do. do. 68 ,,

Total..13871 acres.
Fallow and cleared.. 9613

Total increase ..23484 or 171 per cent.

The increase in Districts has been,—

DISTRICT.	WHEAT. Increase in Acres.	INCREASE OF TOTAL CULTIVATION INCLUDING FALLOWED AND CLEARED LAND. Acres.
Murray	253	479
Perthshire	636	2656
Plantagenet	275	855
Sussex	424	1588
Toodyay	2084	5324
Victoria	1432	4756
Wellington	1034	2548
Yorkshire	1575	5279
Total....	7713	23484

With respect to the yield of Wheat in 1859, averaging the Crop at the low net yield of 12 bushels to the acre gives 163320 bushels ; and, supposing each person in the population of 14837 consumes 8 bushels per annum or 118696 bushels, and allowing 24,000 bushels for seed leaves a surplus of 20624 bushels, which, at 45 bushels to the ton of 2000 lbs., equals nearly 459 tons.

With regard to Agriculture in 1854, there were 1395 employed therein on 13715 acres of cultivated land (including fallowed and cleared) or nearly 10 acres to each man, in 1859 there were 2637 employed on 37,137 acres or about 14 acres to each man.

Western Australia has great capabilities for the production of grain, especially in the Northern Districts, where little or no outlay is necessary for clearing; I allude more particularly to the Greenough Flats : there is also a very large extent of alluvial flats in the Southern Districts not to be surpassed for the growth of corn, by any land in the Colony.

During 1859, 20833 gallons of Colonial Wine were made and 18952 lbs. of Dried Fruits.

The cultivation of Vineyards is gradually on the increase, and there is every reason to believe that Western Australia is well adapted for the growth of the Vine and will become an Exporting Wine Country. At the present time Light Wines are produced that would find a ready market in England, and it is expected that when persons are introduced into the Colony who understand the Manufacture of Wine, the Western Australian Wines will prove most remunerative to the Vineyard Proprietors in the Colony.

STOCK.

The number of Stock in 1859, was :—

Horses.	Cattle.	Sheep.	Pigs.
8386	30990	234815	11430

Shewing an increase on 1854 of—

	Horses.	Cattle.	Sheep.	Pigs.
Increase	3710	10713	61572	7988
Per cent. about	80	53	36	232
Average annual per centage	16	10·6	7·2	46·4

The consumption of Stock for food so far as can be ascertained was in 1859—

Cattle   6300
Sheep   39000

and 517000 lbs. of Pork, Bacon and Hams salted and cured in the Colony.

Averaging Cattle at 500 lbs., and Sheep at 40 lbs., with the addition of Colonial Pork as above, together with 117000 lbs. of imported meats, this would give the annual consumption in 1858, 5,314,000.

Taking the number of Meat consumers to be 14000, this gives the very large daily average of 1lb. 2 oz. to each person, but then a considerable portion of this is taken by the Ships in the various ports.

I may mention here that 5,242,500 acres are leased as Stock Runs, to which add say, at least 1,300,000 acres in Fee Simple not cultivated, and capable of feeding stock, gives 6,543,500 acres, and averaging 300 acres as capable of feeding 20 Sheep, 4 head of Cattle, and 1 Horse, there is at present under Fee and Lease, sufficient run for nearly 436,000 Sheep, 88,000 Cattle, and 22,000 Horses.

CROWN LANDS.

The following table shews the sale of Crown Lands from 1854 to 1859, inclusive :—

CROWN LANDS GRANTED AND SOLD IN ACRES.

DISTRICT.	1854	1855	1856	1857	1858	1859
Avon	461	372	660¼	170	314	371
Canning	110	..	10	60	10	10
Cockburn Sound	70	227	207	72	127	192
Hay	..	..	..	10	..	10
Helena	..	..	10	10	..	..
Kent	..	..	20	..	20	..
Kojonup	..	30	50	..	65	140
Lakes	50	..	3¾	..	..	..
Murray	20	66	303	..	..	..
Murchison	100	100	..	120	..	..
Melbourne	110	60	157	221	296	10
Nelson	..	..	10	30	70	147
Plantagenet	225	184	32	20	20	..
Sussex	65	40	118½	120	20	40
Swan	114	184	182	137	75	223
Victoria	485	207	436	1670¾	2333	910
Wellington	322	200	256½	72¼	8	129
Williams	10	45	..	..	10	50
Total	2142	1715	2456¼	2713	3368	2232

Thus of the 8313 acres purchased during the last three years, 5034 acres or 60 per cent. were in Victoria, and 1316 acres or 16 per cent. in York and Toodyay Districts.

In remarking on the granting and purchase of Crown Lands, I would take the opportunity of referring to all the Regulations under which Lands have been granted and sold in Western Australia, the Returns having been kindly furnished me by Mr. Hillman, the Acting Surveyor General.

In 1827, Sir James Stirling (then Capt. Stirling, R.N.) made so favorable a report of the capabilities of the Country adjacent to the Swan River that the Home Government who had been previously impressed with the importance of forming a settlement on the West Coast of the Australian continent, determined to do so in that vicinity, but from the objection people had to emigrate thereto, the Authorities were obliged to hold out inducements in the granting of land as favorable as they imagined they well could be, and the first regulations under Colonial Circular A, dated 5th December, 1828 were to the effect that although it was the intention of Her Majesty's Government to form a settlement on the West Coast of Australia, they did not intend to incur any expense in conveying settlers, or in supplying them with necessaries after their arrival; such persons however, as might be prepared to proceed there at their own cost before the end of the year 1829, in parties comprehending a proportion of not less than 5 Females to 6 Male settlers would receive grants of land in fee simple (free of Quit Rents) proportioned to the Capital they might invest upon public or private objects in the Colony, to the satisfaction of Her Majesty's Government at Home, certified by the Officer Administering the Colonial Government at the rate of one acre for every 1s. 6d. of the Capital so invested, provided they gave previous security, firstly that all supplies sent to the Colony, whether of provisions, stores, or other articles, which might be purchased there or which should have been sent out for the use of them, or their parties, on the requisition of the Secretary of State, if not paid for on delivery in the Colony, should be paid for at home, such capitalist being held liable in his proportion, and 2udly, that in the event of the Establishment being broken up by the Government, all persons desirous of returning to the British Islands should be conveyed to their own homes at the expense of the Capitalists, by whom they may have been taken out. The passages of laborers and servants, whether paid for by themselves or others, and whether they were Male or Female, provided the proportion of the sexes before mentioned were retained, were to be considered as an investment of Capital, entitling such party by whom such payment may have been made to an allowance of land at the rate of £15 or 200 acres for the passage of every such laborer or servant, over and above any other investment of Capital.

Any land thus granted which should not have been brought into cultivation or otherwise improved or reclaimed from its wild state to the satisfaction of the Colonial Government within 21 years from the date of the Grant in occupation should at the end of the 21 years revert to the Crown.

Under these regulations 421,340 acres are now in Fee Simple, and 11660 acres are still subject to location duty, 20,000 having been surrendered or have reverted to the Crown.

The original Grants under Circular A were, to

Mr. Peel................................ 250,000
Colonel Latour 103,000
Sir Jas. Stirling....................... 100,000

These Regulations were superseded by Colonial Office Circular B, dated 13th January, 1829, which after recapitulating the first portion of Circular A (with the exception that it only extended to parties who might arrive in the Colony before the end of 1830) stated provision would be made by Law for rendering those Capitalists who might be engaged in taking out laboring persons liable for the future maintenance of those persons, should they from infirmity or other cause be unable to maintain themselves; and further stated that the settler to be entitled to his Fee Simple would have to expend at the least 1s. 6d. per acre on the land in Stock, Implements, Husbandry, or in the cultivation of the land, or in solid improvements such as buildings, roads, or other works of the kind. Article 6 of Circular B states "that " any land thus allotted, of which a fair proportion of at least ¼ shall not have been brought " into cultivation or otherwise improved to the satisfaction of the Local Government within 3 " years from the date of the License of Occupation, shall, at the end of 3 years be liable to " one further payment of 6d. per acre for all land not so cultivated or improved to be paid

"into the Public Chest of the Settlement; and at the expiration of 7 years more, so much of
"the whole grant as shall still remain in an uncultivated state shall revert absolutely to the
"Crown, and in every grant will be contained a condition that at any time within 10 years
"from the date thereof the Government can resume uncultivated lands for Public purposes
"without compensation."

From Circulars A and B, it is apparent that the Government in making large grants of land
to individuals intended that those lands should be all improved by Cultivation, within 21 years
in the first instance and 10 years in the other, but subsequently these regulations were con-
strued to mean that if improvements and expenditure for stock to the value of $\frac{1}{2}$ the improvements required, amounted in the whole to 1s. 6d. per acre, the holder of the land was entitled
to his Fee Simple.

On 10th July, 1830, a third Circular, C, was issued from the Colonial Office to affect persons
emigrating to the Colony, subsequently to December, 1830, granting land at the rate of one
acre for every 3s. of capital invested, and 100 acres for any laborer or servant introduced,
thus doubling the nominal price of Crown Lands, and the limit for improvements was reduced
to 4 years, with a fine of 1s. per acre if not so improved in 2 years, and a reversion to the
Crown if not improved to the full extent at the end of the 4 years.

Under Circulars B and C, 1,157,048 acres in 490 grants were assigned in occupancy of
which 144,432 acres have been resumed and 316,749 acres have been surrendered to the
Crown, and 642,124 have been granted in Fee, and 53,743 acres in 7 grants still remain
subject to location duties, being 1 grant of 5000 acres in the Sussex District, and 6 grants of
48,743 acres in the Wellington District belonging to the Western Australian Company.

On 1st March, 1831, a fourth Colonial Office Circular, D appeared, doing away with all
free grants, excepting those to Officers in the Army and Navy selling out or retiring on half-
pay, for the purpose of settling, and for the introduction of labor, and authorizing the sale in
Fee Simple of Crown Lands at the minimum rate of 5s. per acre.

In consequence of the very near failure of the Colony in the first instance of its Establishment, the Government took a very liberal view as to enforcing the fines for non-improvement,
and allowed parties desirous of obtaining their Fee Simples without the performance of any
location duties, to do so on surrendering land at 1s. 6d. per acre, which was paid for in remission Tickets at 5s. per acre—that is, for 10 acres of land surrendered, they were allowed either
a remission of 3 acres in future purchases, or they might take up in fee 3 acres of the lands
already assigned in occupancy.

Under this regulation 316,749 acres of land were surrendered entitling the Settlers to 95025
acres in Fee.

In July 1841 under authority of the Secretary of States' despatch, No. 10 of 13th March,
1841, the price of land was raised to 12s. per acre, and but few sales were made at that price,
viz., 6174 acres in 10 grants—nearly the whole of which was paid for by remission Tickets.

On 3rd June, 1841, it was notified under directions of the Secretary of State, dated 23rd
March, 1841, that the minimum price of Crown Lands was to be raised to £1 per acre—this
was carried into effect by Notice dated 17th June, 1841, of Regulations under which lands
were to be purchased from the Crown, which provided that Land was to be sold in blocks of
not less than 160 acres, and the Fee Simple owners of all of these blocks were to be entitled
to a commonage immediately adjoining their land so long as such adjacent lands was vacant.
This arrangement was not approved by the Home Government, and on 19th July, 1842, it
was notified that the minimum quantity that could be purchased from the Crown was 320
acres, without any right of Commonage.

On the 27th March, 1843, the Land Sales' Act 5th and 6th Vict., Cap. 36 was proclaimed
as being in force in Western Australia. Under the provisions of which a new set of Regulations was promulgated on June 14th, 1843, stating that land would be Sold by Auction in
sections of not less than 160 acres, and not more than 640 acres at an upset price of £1 per
acre, with the exception of "Special Country Lots" which were to be from 20 to 160 acres
each and subject to such upset price as the Government thought fit; and further, persons
might buy blocks of 20,000 acres or more by making special application.

It will be unnecessary for me to notice many unimportant alterations made in these Regulations, but shall state the provision of those to come into operation in April, 1860, viz. :—

Lands at the disposal of the Crown shall be distinguished into four separate classes, namely, as Town, Suburban, Country and Mineral Lands.

No Waste Lands shall be sold for a less price than ten shillings per acre. Town and Suburban Lots shall be sold by Public Auction, Country Lots at a fixed price of ten shillings per acre ; and lands known or supposed to contain Minerals shall be offered for Sale by Public Auction as " Mineral Lots" at an upset price of not less than twenty shillings per acre.

The size and upset prices of Town and Suburban Lots shall be fixed from time to time by the Governor. The minimum size of Country and Mineral Lots to be 40 acres.

Any smaller quantity than 40 acres of Country or Mineral Land, laid out for Sale, or applied for under special circumstances, shall be sold at such additional price as each case may seem to justify.

Mineral lots shall be paid for by depositing one-third of the purchase money at the time of purchase , and the purchaser shall contract to pay one-third more on the first day of January next but one following the day of Sale, and the balance together with the Fee for Title Deed and Enrolment, on the same day in the succeeding year. Failure in making either of the last two payments shall involve forfeiture of the land, and of all deposits and improvements.

With regard to the Leasing of Crown Lands, the following table shews the number of acres in each year since 1852, previous to which year, although the system of Leasing Crown Land existed but few persons availed themselves of it, and to but a small extent.

CROWN LANDS LEASED SINCE 1852 IN ACRES.

YEAR.	CLASS A	CLASS B	TILLAGE	TOTAL
	ACRES.	ACRES.	ACRES.	ACRES.
1852	358267	1997572	400	2356239
1853	274239	2275900	400	2649729
1854	400926	2449232	600	2849758
1855	424927	3122477	2020	3549424
1856	419871	3708977	2520	4128848
1857	535318	3974084	3035	4512437
1858	574748	4383562	6736	4965046
1859	566763	4668322	7401	5242486

The first Regulations for Leasing and Licensing of Crown Lands were published on 9th May, 1838, and provided that blocks of not less than 640 acres would be put up to Public Auction at a minimum of £1 for each square mile, the Lease to be an Annual one, and lands could be sold out of the land comprised therein on giving one months' notice to the lessee.

On 21st July, 1843, provision was made that all leases would be put up to Public Auction in blocks of not less than 640 acres, excepting in very special cases, that a deposit of 10 per cent. be made on application, and the License only to continue for one year.

On 17th October, 1844 other regulations were issued under provision of the Local Ordinance 7th Vict., No. 14, by which the minimum quantity of licensed land was 4000 acres for depasturing stock, and they were no longer put up to Auction, but granted on the following terms :

Not exceeding 1000 sheep, 4000 acres £10.

    ,,   1500 ,,   6000 ,,   12.

    ,,   2000 ,,   8000 ,,   14.

    ,,   3000 ,, 12000 ,,   16.

Each horse or head of horned cattle being reckoned equal to 4 sheep.

On 6th October, 1849, the following scale of License Fees was established :—

For 6000 acres, £10 per annum and £1 per thousand for any additional quantity up to 20,000 acres. No license to be issued for a greater quantity in one block than 20,000 acres.

Up to 31st December, 1849, Fee Simple proprietors had a preferable right to rent the Crown Lands adjoining to their Freeholds, but from that date such priority was not acknowledged.

On the 1st November, 1851, by Authority of an Order in Council, dated 22d March, 1850, and published on 31st December, 1850, Crown Lands were leased under the following Regulations.

Lands to be divided into two Classes, A and B. The Leases under Class A to be but for one year.

Under Class B the leases were to be for 8 years, at an annual rent of £5, with 10s. additional for each thousand acres comprised in the lease, and the Governor had power to exclude from the computation any part of the land reported to him by the proper Officer to be unavailable for pastoral purposes ; at the end of each year portions of the leased lands might be sold, subject to pre-emption by the Lessee, who possessed that right at all times during the Currency of his Lease.

Leases were subject to renewal for a period of 8 years.

Class A was defined to be land within 2 miles of the sea coast, three miles from the outer boundary of any occupied Townsite or any land within one mile of any Fee Simple Land, and within two miles of the banks of certain rivers and inlets.

Class B comprehended all other Lands in the Colony open for selection.

Leases were subject to forfeiture in three modes.

1st. Upon any conviction for Felony against the Lessee.

2nd. Upon conviction for any offence against the Law by the Lessee, to be enquired into by any two or more Justices of the Peace within 3 months after such conviction, and if the forfeiture be recommended by such Justices the Governor's confirmation was required before it could be carried into effect.

Without noticing many minor alterations which have taken place since 1851, I proceed to state the provisions of the New Regulations which are to come into force in April, 1860.

All Waste Crown Lands are to be divided into two classes A and B.

Class A comprehends all Waste Crown Lands comprised within the following boundaries, with the exception of such lands within the same boundaries as shall be, at the date of these Regulations coming into force, comprised within Class B or Tillage Leases, held under Authority of the Order in Council, dated 22nd March, 1850, viz. :—

On the South, by the right bank of the Blackwood River upwards from Flinders' Bay to its junction with the Tweed River, thence, up the right bank of the said Tweed River, a a distance of ten miles in a direct line from said junction, thence in a direct line to the centre of Kojonup Spring ; on the East by a direct line from the centre of Kojonup Spring aforesaid, to the summit of County Peak ; thence by a line about twenty miles in length in the direction of North 27° 30' West, to the summit of Wongon Hills, thence by a North line about thirty four miles in length, thence by a West line drawn through a spot twenty miles North from the centre of Dundaraga Spring, thence by a North line, to a spot five miles East from the Coal Seam, near the Irwin River, thence by a West line five miles in length to the said Coal Seam, and thence by a direct line to the great Southern bend of the Murchison River, next below the Geraldine Mine ; on the North by a West line from the great bend of the Murchison River aforesaid to the Sea Coast, and on the West by the Sea Coast between the South and North boundaries above described. All bearings above given being true.

Class A shall also comprehend all such lands within the above boundaries that are now in Class B leases, which may determine otherwise than by efflux of time.

Class A land shall further comprehend all lands outside the above boundaries, which may be within the distance of one mile from any lands which may be in fee simple outside the same boundaries at the time when these regulations shall come into force, with the exception of lands purchased within leases in Class B.

Class B comprehends all other lands of the Colony open for selection.

Within the limits of Class A Pastoral Leases may be granted for one year at a yearly rent of 2s. per 100 acres for sections of 1000 acres and upwards ; the land comprised in such lease being at all times open for purchase ; the purchasers of any such land having a right of commonage at the rate of 10 head of horned cattle or horses for every 40 acres purchased, and 5 head for every additional 20 acres.

Holders of Land in Fee Simple of not less than 10 acres around whose land a Class A lease may be taken to have the same right of commonage.

Within the limits of Class B Pastoral Leases may be granted for any term not exceeding 8 years, at a rent of £5 per annum with 10s. additional per annum for each 1000 acres. No one lease to be for more than 10000 acres.

Lessees to have a pre-emptive right to purchase within his lease at 10s. per acre, any portion of land (not being less than 40 acres, or not containing minerals) during the first year of his lease, and also to select within 3 years for a homestead a block not exceeding one-fiftieth part of his run.

After the first year the unbought portion of the lease (excepting the selection for a homestead reserved as above for 3 years) the land to be open for public purchase, and the purchasers to be entitled to the same commonage as in Class A.

The Pastoral Licenses and Leases in Class A and B do not permit the occupants of Land to cultivate any portion thereof for cereal productions, but the Local Government of this Colony fully appreciating the great advantage and importance of establishing small Farms and Agricultural Stations as a means of permanent occupation of the land and of increasing our production of bread stuffs and other grain so as to be independent of Foreign Importations, proposed a scheme for granting Tillage Leases for any quantity of Land not exceeding 320 acres, and at a Rent not less than 2s. per acre per annum with right of pre-emption and other privileges. This proposal was confirmed and embraced in the Order of Council of the 22d March, 1850, and commenced operation concurrently with the other regulations for the occupation of Crown Lands in 1852. From that date to the present time there has been a steady and latterly a rapid development of the resources of the Country in this branch of Rural industry, as is indicated by the following particulars shewing the quantity of Land held under such Leases in each year, viz. :—

In 1852	400	acres.
„ 1853	400	„
„ 1854	600	„
„ 1855	2020	„
„ 1856	2520	„
„ 1857	3035	„
„ 1858	6736	„
„ 1859	7401	„

These Tillage Regulations have been highly successful, and have been prominently instrumental in raising this Colony to a condition of independence, for previously to the year 1858 a large amount of Capital was annually expended in the importation of Flour and Horse corn, without any equivalent exchange to prevent the impoverishing effect of such a state of the market ; but principally owing to the encouragements thus given to agriculture the proceedings of the past year have realized the important fact that for the first time we have become independent of foreign supply, with a certain prospect of having, in the course of the present year a surplus quantity for export.

As the prosperity of a country must depend on its capability of production, it is a subject of great gratification that in so important an article as the staff of life we are become self-supporting.

The system of granting Tillage Leases is confined I believe to Western Australia, and its operation having been so successful, it has been thought advisable to continue it in the New Land Regulations which come into operation on the 15th of April, 1860, not only without any restriction of privileges, but with the additional advantage of a reduction of rent to one-half.

TIMBER LICENSES.

The Regulations to come into force under the New Land Regulations for leasing lands for felling timber are—

Application for a pair of Sawyers, Splitters or Cutters, to fell, cut, split and remove, any timber, sandal, jam, fire or other wood growing or being on any Waste Lands of the Crown in Western Australia, shall be made to the Collector or to any Sub-Collector of Revenue, or to any Resident Magistrate, who shall thereupon issue the required License, after payment in advance of the following fees:—

For any quantity of land not exceeding 640 acres . . . .£20 per annum,

Exceeding 640 and not exceeding 1280 acres 40   do.

Or 10 shillings per month for each pair of Sawyers.

To cut Sandal Wood £2 10s. for each pair of Sawyers, and £1 15s. for each additional man employed

No such license shall be issued for a period less than one nor more than six months. The names of the parties applying for a license shall be inserted therein, and no such license shall be transferable.

Applications for special licenses to fell, remove and sell the timber growing and being on any particular Waste Lands, shall be addressed to the Surveyor General by letter, fully describing the quantity, position and boundaries of the land required, and the date from which a license is to commence.

Any such application shall be accompanied by a deposit of £5 or by the receipt of any Collector of Revenue for that amount. The land applied for shall be selected and described according to the rules laid down in Chapter 5 of the Regulations as published in the Government Gazette of 14th February, 1860.

Such license as last aforesaid shall be prepared in the Office of the Surveyor General, and shall be deliverable by any Collector of Revenue, or by the Resident Magistrate of any District in which the land may be situated, on payment of any balance due thereon.

Every such license shall be for 12 Calendar Months; and if not taken up at Albany within 2 Calendar months, or at Perth and other Districts within one Calendar month from the date of deposit, the license shall be forfeited, together with the deposit, and the land shall be open to fresh applicants. The License shall not be transferrable.

No rights or privileges shall be conveyed by any such License, beyond those of felling, cutting up, and removing any indigenous timber growing or being on the land licensed; and at the expiration of the license, all timber left on the ground shall be the property of the Government, unless otherwise arranged by special application in writing, addressed to the Colonial Secretary, or by a renewal of the license for a further term to which an existing lessee shall be considered to have a preferable claim.

POST OFFICE.

The following is taken from a Return of the number of Letters and Newspapers passed through the General Post Office during the three years ended the 31st December, 1859, furnished me by Mr. Helmich, the Postmaster General.

	1857.	1858.	1859.
Inland Letters received and forwarded	70084	83120	115806
Letters from places out of the Colony received	12022	16895	17346
Letters to places out of the Colony forwarded	13416	16765	21290
Total letters received and forwarded	95222	116780	154442

POST OFFICE—*continued.*

	1857.	1858.	1859.
Colonial newspapers forwarded in the Colony,..........	34094	36116	36251
Colonial newspapers forwarded out of the Colony	4038	6727	8266
Newspapers received from places out of the Colony ..	18936	25784	33737
Total newspapers received and forwarded	57068	68627	78254
Registered letters forwarded to places out of the Colony (included in the above return)	373	692	771
Letters forwarded *via* Marseilles and Trieste (included in the above return)	563	801	1382

In addition to the above I would add that in 1859 as compared with 1854—

The increase of the number of Inland Letters received in and forwarded from the General Post Office, Perth, was } 58000 or nearly 100 per cent.

Of Foreign Letters received and forwarded............ 19236 or nearly 100 per cent.

The total number of Letters passing through the General Post Office as above and through the District Post Offices in 1859 was about 12 to each of the Population.

The distance travelled during 1859 by the Mail Carriers not including Expresses and Town deliveries was nearly 61,000 miles ; and the expense of the Conveyance of the Mails (irrespective of the Subsidy to Royal Mail Service) was about 2¼d. on each letter or newspaper, or about 5¼d. per mile.

BIRTHS.

The number of Births in 1859 were 531, of which 269 were Males and 262 Females, being in proportion of 10 to 280 of the whole population ; 10 Male Births to 357 of the Male Population, and 10 female births to 203 of the female population, the proportion of male births to female was 100 to 98, and of Female to Male births 100 to 103.

The Proportion of Births to Deaths was as 100 to 39 ; of Male Births to Male Deaths as 100 to 54 ; of Female Births to Female Deaths as 100 to 25 ; or 100 Deaths to 254 Births in the whole population ; 10 Male Deaths to 19 Male Births ; and 10 Female Deaths to 40 Female Births.

The excess of Births over Deaths was 322 ; of Male Births over Male Deaths, 126 ; and of Female Births over Female Deaths 196.

The number of Twin Births was 6 or about 1 in every 89 births.

The number of Illegitimate Births was 14 or about 1 in every 39 Births.

The number of Still Born Children was 8 or about 1 in every 67 Births.

The number of Married Women under 48 years of age living with their husbands was 1532, and deducting 14 illegitimate births there was about 1 birth to every 3 Married Women capable of bearing children, and thus out of every 100 of these Women 66 did not bear children during 1859 ; the average annual Proportion during the last 5 years has been about 38 births to every 100 Married Women under 48 years of age.

The natural increase of Population on 31st December, 1859, since 1833 by excess of Births over Deaths has been 3800, and the total increase was 13184, therefore the increase in the 25 years by excess of Immigration over Emigration has been 9384.

DEATHS.

The number of Deaths in 1859 were 209—being 143 Males and 66 Females, or 1 in 71, or 1·4 per cent of the whole population ; 1 Male in 63 or 1·5 per cent. of the Male population, and 1 Female in nearly 81 or 1·2 per cent. of the Female population ; the Male Deaths to Female Deaths were as 100 to 46, and the Female to the Male Deaths as 100 to 216.

The following were the Ages at Death in 1859 :—

	MALES.	FEMALES.	TOTAL.
Under 1	47	37	84
1 to 3	11	6	17
3 to 5	..	..	..
Total under 5	58	43	101
5 to 20	9	3	12
20 to 40	44	12	56
40 to 60	25	6	31
60 & upwards	7	2	9
Total above 5	85	23	108
Totals	143	66	209

THE CAUSES OF DEATH WERE—

	MALES.	FEMALES.	TOTAL.
Accident and Violence	28	4	32
Heart Disease	6	1	7
Disease of Lungs	9	2	11
Do. of Brain	5	2	7
Child Birth	..	3	3
Disease of Bowels	29	14	43
Decline	10	7	17
Convulsions	21	15	36
Still Born	3	5	8
All other causes	32	13	45
	143	66	209

Thus in 1859 of the 209 Deaths 101 or 48·3 per cent. were under 5 years of age, of whom 58 were Males or 40·5 per cent. of Male Deaths, and 43 Females or 65·1 per cent. of Female Deaths.

The annual average of Deaths in Western Australia has been, from 1833 to 1849 inclusive, 1·06 per cent. ; 1850 to 1859 inclusive, ·85 per cent.

The following Table shews the Ages at Death from the specified causes during the six years from 1854 to 1859, both years inclusive.

Thus it will be seen the ages at Death during the last six years have been :—

	MALES.	FEMALES.	TOTAL.
Under 1	145	104	249
1 to 5	37	39	76
Total under 5	182	143	325
5 to 20	23	14	37
20 to 40	169	46	215
40 and upwards	114	35	149
Total above 5	306	95	401

The number of Births during the last 7 years were 2951—and 10 in every 118 died before the expiration of the first year after birth, or about 8¼ per cent.

The causes of death in children under 1 were as follow in the last 6 years :—

	MALES.	FEMALES.	TOTAL.
Anasarca	1	—	1
Accident	2	4	6
Atrophy	6	6	12
Brain, diseases of	8	2	10
Bowels do.	37	30	67
Convulsions	53	28	81
Consumption	—	1	1
Fever	1	2	3
Hooping Cough	3	3	6
Lungs, diseases of	12	5	17
Lockjaw	—	1	1
Malformation	—	3	3
Stillborn	14	14	28
Teething	3	3	6
Throat, disease of	4	2	6
Found dead	1	—	1
Totals	145	104	249

The number of still-born children were 5 in every 107 births or a little more than 1 per cent. Of the above 249 deaths of children under 1 year old—

About 1 in every 50 was from accident and violence,

About 1 in every 22 from Atrophy,

About 1 in every 25 from Brain disease,

About 10 in every 37 from disease of Bowels,

About 1 in every 3 from Convulsions,

About 1 in every 83 from Fever,

About 1 in every 41 from Hooping Cough,

About 2 in every 29 from Lung disease,

About 1 in every 83 from Malformation,

About 1 in every 41 from Teething,

About 1 in every 41 from disease of the Throat, and

About 10 in every 89 were Stillborn.

Thus during the last six years the number of deaths of children under 1 year old were 249, or about 10 in 29 of the whole number of deaths, or about 34 per cent. ; between 1 and 3 62 or about 10 in every 117 deaths or nearly 9 per cent. Deaths between 3 and 5 were 14 or about 10 in 516 deaths or nearly 2 per cent—under 3 there were 311 or about 10 in 23 deaths or nearly 43 per cent., and the total number under 5 years of age was 325 or about 10 in 22 deaths, or nearly 45 per cent.

Of the 76 deaths between 1 and 5, 4 were from Atrophy ; 8 were from Brain disease ; 21 were from disease of the Bowels ; 12 were from accident ; 4 from Croup ; 6 from Convulsions, 10 from disease of the Lungs, and 11 from other causes.

Between 5 and 20 there were but 37 deaths or about 1 in 20 of the whole number or about 5 per cent.

Of these, 10 were from Accident ; 7 from Diseases of Brain ; 5 from Bowel complaint ; and 7 from Decline ; and 8 from other causes.

Between 20 and 40 there were 215 Deaths, or about 5 in 17 of the whole number, or nearly 30 per cent—of these 45 were from accident and violence ; 14 from disease of Bowels ; 41 from Decline ; 14 from Fever ; 35 from disease of Lungs, and 66 from other causes.

Of 4 0 years of age and upwards there were 149 deaths, or about 10 in 49 or about 20 per cent—of these 13 were from Accident and Violence; 10 from Bowel complaint; 18 from Decline; 27 from Debility; 12 from Heart disease; 14 from disease of the Lungs, and 55 from other causes.

During the last 6 years 88 persons lost their lives by Accident or Violence, or rather more than one-eighth of the whole number of Deaths, or about 12 per cent, thus :—

Burned 7; Drowned 39; Suicide 4; Murdered 6; Hanged 6; thrown from Horse 6; killed by Bullocks 1; Suffocated 2; Killed in Stone Quarry 1; Shot by accident 1; Run Over by Cart 1; causes not stated, 14.

Of the total number of persons who have died in the Colony during the last six years, 35 died from Brain diseases, (of whom 18 were under 5 years of age) or about 5 per cent.; 117 of Diseases of Bowels (of whom 88 were under 5 years of age) or about 16 per cent; 87 of Convulsions, all of whom were under 5 years of age, or about 12 per cent.; 69 of decline (of whom 3 were under 5 years of age) or nearly 10 per cent.; 33 of Debility, or about 4½ per cent.; 25 of Fever, (of whom 4 were under 5 years of age) or about 3½ per cent.; 23 of Heart Disease, or about 3 per cent.; 76 of diseases of the Lungs (of whom 27 were under 5) or about 10 per cent.

The Colony has been founded 30 years, and the Deaths among those between the ages of 5 and 30 who were born in the Colony have been but 20 during the last six years, namely—

```
          5  to  15   years of age  4
         15  to  20        ..        6
         20  to  30        ..       10
                                   ────
                       Total....    20
```

or about 1 in 7 of the total number of deaths between 5 and 30, or rather more than 2.7 per cent. of the total number of deaths during the last six years.

Of these 20 deaths,

```
          3  were from disease of the brain,
          4  from disease of the Bowels,
          8  from Accident,
          1  from Hooping Cough, and
          4  from decline.
```

With regard to the number of Adults who died from Consumption, Heart Disease, Lung Disease, Liver Complaints and Chronic diseases of the Bowels, with very few exceptions the seeds of these complaints were brought with them into the Colony.

In connexion with this subject I append a list of cases treated in the Colonial Hospital, Perth, during the last 3 years, obligingly furnished me by Mr. Ferguson, the Colonial Surgeon.

RETURN of the number of Diseases treated in the Colonial Hospital, Perth, from 1st January. 1857, to 31st December, 1859.

DISEASES.	NUMBER OF CASES TREATED.	NUMBER OF DEATHS.
General Chronic Disease ..	4	2
Febris Ephemera	8	..
„ Gastrica	2	2
„ Intermittens	1	..
Scrofula..	3	..
Scorbutus	3	..
Rheumatism Acute and Chronic	38	..
Observatio	3	..
Cephalalgia	3	..
Coup de Soleil	1	..
Paralysis	7	1
Mania	2	..
Dementia	7	1
Delirium Tremens	1	..
Pericarditis	1	1
Disease of Heart	4	1
Pneumonia	8	1

Continued.

Diseases.	Number of Cases Treated.	Number of Deaths.
Phthisis Pulmonalis	8	4
Pleuritis	2	
Inflamed Throat	1	
Dyspepsia	18	
Diarrhœa	3	
Dysentery, Acute and Chronic	11	3
Torpor, Intestinorum	4	
Chronic disease of Liver	4	1
Peritonitis	1	
Ascites	4	1
Anasarca	1	
Albuminuria	2	1
Dysuria	1	
Tænia	1	
Abscesses in various situations	11	
Lumbar Abscess	1	1
Ulcers in various situations	24	
Ulcerated Absorbments	1	1
Inflamed Leg	4	
Incised Wounds	7	
Gun Shot Wounds	3	
Extensive Lacerations of Face and removal of inferior Maxilla	1	
Injury of Knee	9	
Contusions	3	
Burn	2	1
Gonorrhœa	3	
Syphilis	11	
Disease of Knee Joint	1	
„ Elbow	2	
„ Spine	1	
Necrosis of Clavicle	1	

Continued.

Diseases.	Number of Cases Treated.	Number of Deaths.
Non-union of Fractured Leg	1	..
Fracture of Thigh	3	..
,, Leg	1	..
Fracture of Thigh and compound fracture of Leg ..	1	1
Fracture of Ribs	1	..
Dislocation of Elbow. . ..	1	..
Ophthalmia (various character)	36	..
Amaurosis	1	..
Ozœna	1	..
Ranula	1	..
Fistula	2	..
Hemorrhoids..	1	..
Hernia	7	..
Scirrhus of Uterus	2	..
Whitlow, Amputation of Finger	3	..
Amputation of Leg	3	..
Total in the 3 years ..	307	22

CLIMATE.

The Climate of Western Australia is one of the first in the World—the heat of summer is tempered by the sea breezes, and there are but few days during the year of really hot weather, caused by the land wind blowing across bush fires.

The seasons are but three—Spring, from April to June—Winter from June to September and Summer from September to April—the year being thus equally divided into the Rainy and Summer seasons—Spring succeeding Summer and preceding Winter.

There are not any Endemic diseases in Western Australia—an Epidemic Catarrh called the " Influenza" attacks the Colonist twice in the year, at the changes of the season, from Summer to Spring, and Winter to Summer ; this takes the form of a common cold, and is generally very mild in its attacks excepting among the Aborigines, with whom, from their exposed lives it is sometimes fatal—it is uncertain as to the locality of its breaking out, but whenever and wherever it does appear it invariably runs through the whole length and breadth of the Colony, attacking even isolated stations in the bush.

The total number of charges before Magistrates for Misdemeanors in 1859 were 1805 ; of these 557 were against Free Men, 335 against Expirees and Conditional Pardon Men, 811 against Ticket-of-Leave Men, and 102 against Females.

Of these 1805 charges 1400 were for drunkenness and disorderly conduct or 77·5 per cent. leaving but 405 or 22·5 per cent. for other crimes.

Of the 1400 charges for drunkenness and disorderly conduct—

> 433 were against Free Men.
> 251 „ against Expirees and Conditional Pardon Men.
> 642 „ against Ticket-of-Leave Men, and
> 74 „ against Women.

The proportions of these charges were 10 to every 75 Free Male Adults, 10 to every 46 Expirees and Conditional Pardon Men, and 10 to every 25 Ticket-of-Leave Men.

Exclusive of these 1400 charges there were but—

> In Perth 142 other charges for Misdemeanors.
> „ Fremantle 97
> „ Guildford 29
> „ York 42
> „ Toodyay 18
> „ Bunbury 26
> „ Vasse 24
> „ Albany 20
> „ Victoria 7

Of these—

> 151 were for common assault,
> 3 for Burglary,
> 16 for Housebreaking,
> 9 for Forgery,
> 6 for obtaining money under false pretences,
> 3 for Arson,
> 5 for Cruelty to Animals,
> 28 for Vagrancy,
> 141 for Petty Larceny,
> 10 for Robbery from the Person,
> 1 for Robbery with Violence,
> 4 for Stealing Stock,
> 15 for receiving Stolen Property,
> 2 for Perjury,
> 1 for concealing Birth,
> 1 for Assault with intent to commit Rape,
> 1 for Murder of a Native,
> 1 for Highway Robbery, and
> 7 for other Felonies.

The proportions of these charges were 10 to each 263 Free Male Adults, 10 to every 140 Expirees and Conditional Pardon Men, and 10 to every 95 Ticket-of-Leave Men.

It is not my place to do more than point out that the prevailing crime of the Colony is Drunkenness, and that other crimes are very few indeed, and proportionably less than in any other British Colony—this is a bold assertion to make but I feel convinced the foregoing statistics will bear it out.

The quiet and peace of the Colony must be a subject of congratulation, particularly when it is considered that it is a Penal Settlement ; and I believe that any person reviewing the facts I have given in this report will draw therefrom the conclusion that the Convict system in Western Australia has prospered beyond the most sanguine hopes that could have been entertained by its originators, of its success.

CIVIL COURT.

The following Return shows the progress of business in the Civil Court, during the last four years, irrespective of Incidental Matters, Motions, Writs of Attachment, and Writs of Execution, &c., &c. :—

Civil Court.

		1856.	1857.	1858.	1859.
LAW SIDE.	Plaints issued..	100	88	79	76
	Amounts sued for .. .. .. £	16603 4s. 9d	12652 3s. 10d.	11821 18s. 10d.	5963 18s. 11d.
	Causes brought to Trial	37	48	53	34
	Judgments confessed in Office ..	43	19	13	11
	Sums decreed in Court .. .. £	2066 17s. 5d.	6961 10s. 8d.	2693 16s. 8d.	1513 8s. 2d.
	Sums confessed in Office .. .. £	7105 8s. 1d.	1628 5s. 8d.	2769 12s. 0d.	340 14s. 9d.
	Causes not otherwise prosecuted ..	20	21	33	31
EQUITY SIDE.	Bills Filed	2	3	6	2
INSOLVENCY SIDE.	Petitions Filed	1	1	2	6
	Debts proved and other Liabilities £		116 1s. 10d.	2588 8s. 3d.	4349 5s. 6d.
	Assets realized .. .. .. £			1424 7s. 11d.	4161 13s. 6d.
ECCLESIASTICAL SIDE.	Probates granted	4	6	3	5
	Letters of Administration granted	10	5	4	11
SITTINGS.	Monthly, Weekly, and oftener, as circumstances may require.				
FEES OF COURT.	Fees received and paid to Government .. .. £	89 15s. 9d.	96 8s. 10d.	145 1s. 3d.	272 16s. 0d.

In conclusion of this Report, I trust the statement I made in its commencement as to the prosperity of the Colony has been borne out by the foregoing Statistics. I have shewn an increased Trade, an increased Revenue, and a great increase in Farming operations, and one sure sign of the progress of Western Australia is the general absence of anxiety as to the future : possessed of valuable indigenous articles for export, a large amount of land suited for cultivation, a considerable extent of Mineral Lands, combined with a fine healthy climate, it requires but energy and capital to raise it to an importance to which its Geographical position entitles it.

ALFRED DURLACHER,
Registrar General.

FREMANTLE :—PRINTED BY AUTHORITY AT THE GOVERNMENT PRESS.